This book belongs to …

Adryanna: Hesseltine

From: Aunt MacKenzie

GROLIER
BOOK CLUB EDITION

Dr. Seuss's

ABC

Beginner Books

BIG A
little   a

What begins with A?

3

Aunt Annie's alligator

. . . A . . a . . A

BIG B

little   b

What begins with B?

Barber
baby
bubbles
and a
bumblebee.

9

BIG C

little   c

What begins with C?

Camel on the ceiling
C . . . . c C

BIG D

little   d

David Donald Doo
dreamed
a dozen doughnuts
and
a duck-dog, too.

ABCDE..e..e

ear

egg

elephant

e

e

E

BIG F

little f

F .. f .. F

Four fluffy feathers
on a
Fiffer-feffer-feff.

17

ABCD
EFG

Goat
girl
googoo goggles
G . . . g . . . G

BIG H

little h

Hungry horse.
Hay.

Hen in a hat.
Hooray !
Hooray !

BIG I

little i

i.... i.... i

Icabod
is
itchy.

So am I.

BIG J
little   j

What begins with j?

Jerry Jordan's
jelly jar
and jam
begin that way.

25

BIG K

little   k

Kitten. Kangaroo.

Kick a kettle.
Kite
and a
king's kerchoo.

BIG L

little   l

Little Lola Lopp.
Left leg.
Lazy lion
licks a lollipop.

BIG M

little m

Many mumbling mice
are making
midnight music
in the moonlight . . .

mighty nice

BIG N

little   n

What begins with those?

Nine new neckties
and a nightshirt
and a nose.

O is very useful.
You use it when you say:
"Oscar's only ostrich
oiled
an orange owl today."

ABCD
EFG
HIJK
LMNO

. . .P

Painting pink pajamas.
Policeman in a pail.

Peter Pepper's puppy.
And now
Papa's in the pail.

BIG Q

little   q

What begins with Q ?

The quick
Queen of Quincy
and her
quacking quacker-oo.

QUACK
QUACK

41

BIG R
little r

Rosy Robin Ross.